J. and W. Grimm

SNOW WHITE AND THE SEVEN DWARFS

Illustrations by Baraldi

BARRON'S
Woodbury, New York/London/Toronto/Sydney

Once upon a time, a queen sat sewing at a window framed in black ebony. It was the middle of winter, and snowflakes fell like feathers on the earth. As she sewed and gazed out of the window, the queen pricked her finger. Three drops of blood fell on the snow.

The red blood looked beautiful against the white snow. "Oh!" thought the queen. "How I would love to have a child as white as snow, as red as blood, and as black as ebony!"

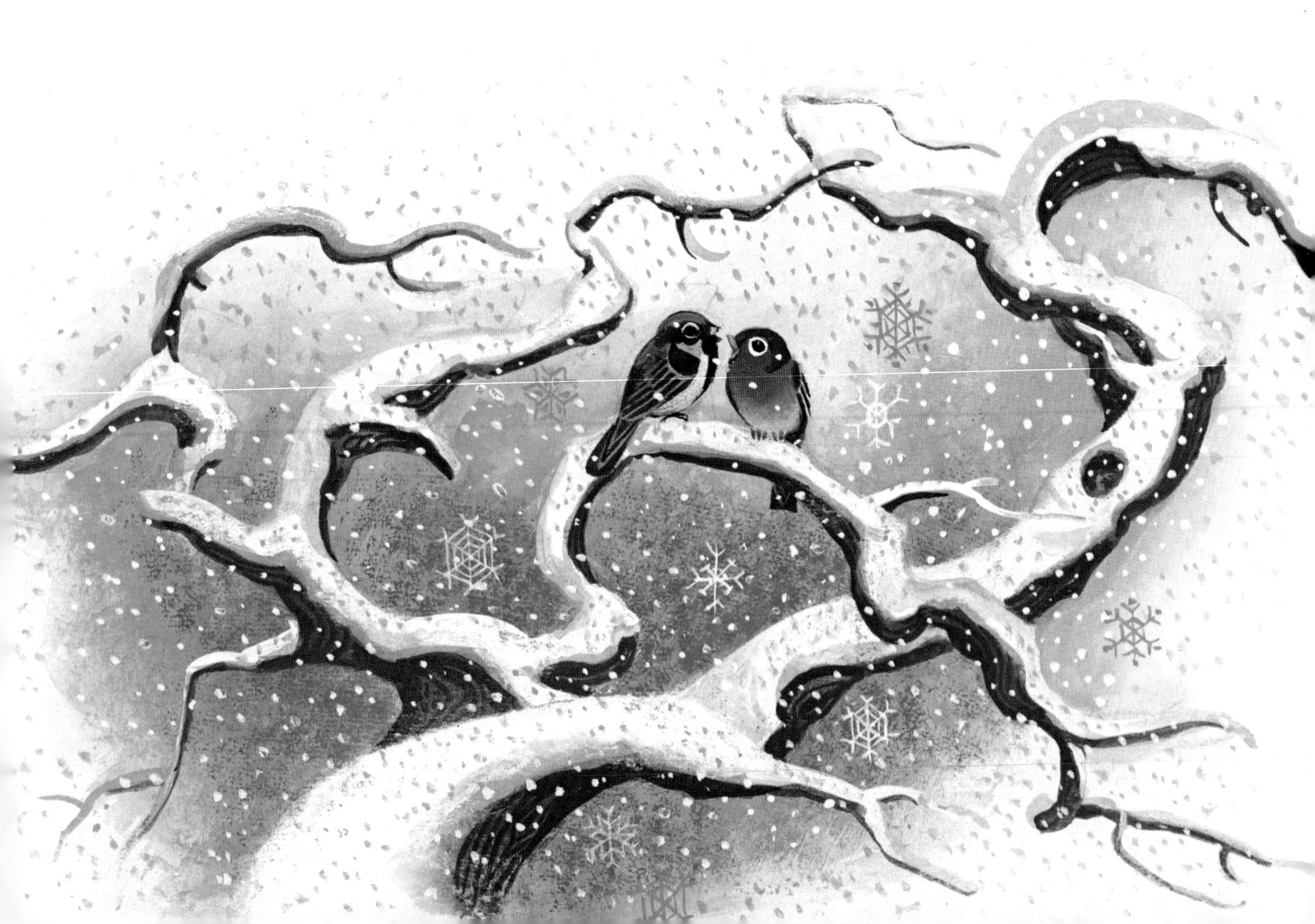

Her wish was granted. Not long afterward, she gave birth to a little girl. The child was beautiful. She had skin as white as snow, lips and cheeks as red as blood, and hair as black as ebony. She was named Snow White. But shortly after Snow White's birth, the good queen died.

A year later, the king married again. His new wife was a beautiful woman, but she was very proud and vain. She couldn't bear to think that anyone in the kingdom might be more beautiful than she.

This new queen had a magic mirror. Every morning she would stand before it, gazing at her own reflection. Then she would ask,

"Mirror, mirror, hanging there,
Who in all the land's most fair?"

And the mirror would always reply,

"My Queen, in all the land I see
None as fine and fair as thee."

This satisfied the queen's proud heart for she knew the mirror always spoke the truth.

But Snow White was growing prettier every day. By the time she was seven years old, she was bright as daylight and lovelier than the queen herself.

The morning came when the queen asked her mirror the usual question, and it replied,

"Your Highness, you are fair, 'tis true,
But Snow White is lovelier than you."

Then the queen flew into a rage. She turned every shade of green in her jealousy, and from that hour she hated Snow White. Her envy, hatred, and malice gave her no peace.

At last she called a hunter to the palace. "Take the child out into the woods," she told him. "Never let me see her face again! Kill her and bring me back her lungs and liver. Then I will know for certain that she is dead."

The hunter did as he was told and led Snow White out into the woods. But as he was drawing out his knife to slay her, she began to weep. “Oh, good hunter, spare my life,” she begged. “I promise to flee into the wild woods and never again return to the palace.”

And because she was so young and beautiful, the hunter had pity on her. "Run along, poor child," he said. And though he thought that the wild beasts would soon eat her up, his heart felt lighter because he hadn't had to kill her himself.

To prove that Snow White was dead, the hunter shot a wild boar and brought its lungs and liver home to the queen. The wicked woman had them cut up and cooked, and then she ate them.

Poor Snow White found herself alone in the wide woods. She was so frightened she didn't know what to do. She began to run. Sharp stones cut her feet, and bramble bushes tore at her clothes. Wild beasts rushed past her, but they did her no harm.

Snow White ran until she saw a little house. Here she stopped to rest, for her tired legs would carry her no further. Inside, everything was very small, but perfectly clean and neat.

On a little table were seven little plates, seven little knives, seven little forks, seven little spoons, and seven little glasses. Side by side against the wall were seven little beds.

Snow White felt so hungry and so thirsty that she ate a bit of bread and a little porridge from each plate, and drank a drop from each glass.

Then, feeling sleepy, she lay down on one of the beds, but it was too short. The second bed was too hard, and the third was too long. Snow White tried all the other beds in turn. Only the seventh one suited her exactly. So she lay down upon it and fell fast asleep.

When darkness fell, the masters of the little house returned. They were seven dwarfs who worked in the mines, down in the heart of the mountain. As soon as they lighted their seven little lamps, they knew that someone had been in the room.

The first said, "Who's been sitting on my little chair?"

The second said, "Who's been picking at my bread?"

The third said, "Who's been tasting my porridge?"

The fourth said, "Who's been eating from my plate?"

The fifth said, "Who's been using my little fork?"

The sixth said, "Who's been cutting with my little knife?"

The seventh said, "Who's been drinking out of my little glass?"

Then the first dwarf looked around and saw a little hollow in his bed. "Who's been lying on my bed?" he asked. The others came running up and cried out, "Someone has been lying in our beds, too."

But when the seventh dwarf came to his bed, his little lantern showed Snow White fast asleep. Quickly he called the others. "Oh, what a beautiful child!" they cried out in wonder and astonishment.

And they were so enchanted that they let her sleep on in the little bed. The seventh dwarf slept an hour with each of his brother dwarfs, and so the night passed.

In the morning, Snow White awoke. When she saw the seven dwarfs, she was frightened. But they spoke to her kindly and asked, “What is your name, child?”

“I am called Snow White,” she replied.

“Why did you come to our house?” the dwarfs then asked.

Snow White told them how her stepmother had wished her put to death, and how the hunter had spared her life. And she told them how she had run the whole day till she came to their little house.

Then the dwarfs said, "Will you stay and keep house for us? Will you cook, make the beds, do the washing, sew and knit? If you will stay, you shall want for nothing."

"Yes," answered Snow White. "I will gladly do all you ask."

And so Snow White came to live with the seven dwarfs.

Every morning the dwarfs went into the mountain to search for gold. Before they left, the good dwarfs warned Snow White, “Beware of your stepmother. She will soon find out you are here. Don’t let anyone into the house.” Snow White promised.

So all day long, Snow White cooked and cleaned and sewed. In the evening, when the dwarfs returned home, Snow White always had supper ready for them.

Now the queen, thinking Snow White had been slain, stepped before her mirror one day. She said,

"Mirror, mirror, hanging there,
Who in all the land's most fair?"

The truthful mirror replied,

"Your Highness, you are fair, 'tis true,
But Snow White is lovelier than you.
In a happy forest glen
She lives with seven little men."

The queen was struck dumb with horror, for the mirror always spoke the truth. She knew now that the hunter had deceived her. Snow White was still alive.

The queen pondered day and night how she might destroy the lovely child. At last she hit upon a plan.

She stained her face and dressed up as an old peddler woman. In this disguise she went through the forest until she came to the house of the seven dwarfs. Then she knocked at the door. "Fine wares to sell," she called out. "Ribbons in all colors!"

Snow White peeped out of the window. Seeing the old woman, she opened the door to buy some of the pretty ribbons.

Suspecting no evil, Snow White let the old woman lace her bodice with the new ribbon. But the old woman pulled so tightly that Snow White fell down as if dead.

In the evening the seven dwarfs came home. How horrified they were when they saw Snow White lying motionless on the floor. They lifted her up tenderly, and when they saw how tightly laced she was, they cut the ribbon. Snow White began to breathe again.

The dwarfs listened as Snow White told them what had happened. "Depend upon it," they said, "the old peddler woman was none other than the queen. In the future you must let no one in if we are not at home."

As soon as the wicked queen got home she went to her mirror and said,

"Mirror, mirror, hanging there,
Who in all the land's most fair?"

The mirror answered as before,

"Your Highness, you are fair, 'tis true,
But Snow White is lovelier than you.
In a happy forest glen
She lives with seven little men."

Enraged, the queen made a poisoned comb. Then she dressed up as another old woman and went through the forest until she reached the house of the seven dwarfs. Knocking on the door, she called out, "Fine combs for beautiful hair!"

She held up the poisoned comb for Snow White to see. It pleased the girl so much that she opened the door. The old woman said, "Now I'll comb your hair properly for you."

Poor Snow White thought no evil. But hardly had the poisoned comb touched her hair than she fell down senseless.

Fortunately it was now near evening. Soon the seven dwarfs returned home. When they saw Snow White, they searched until they found the poisonous comb. The moment they pulled it out of her hair, Snow White came to herself again. Then they warned her once more to be on her guard. She promised to open the door to no one.

As soon as the queen got home she went straight to her mirror. She looked at herself and asked,

"Mirror, mirror, hanging there,
Who in all the land's most fair?"

The mirror answered as before,

"Your Highness, you are fair, 'tis true,
But Snow White is lovelier than you.
In a happy forest glen
She lives with seven little men."

When she heard these words, the queen trembled and shook with rage.

"Snow White shall die," she cried, "even though it cost me my own life."

Then she went to a secret chamber, and there she made a poisonous apple. Outwardly it looked beautiful, white with red cheeks. Everyone who saw it longed to taste it, but anyone who did so would certainly die on the spot. When the apple was ready, the queen stained her face and dressed up as an old peasant woman once again. Then she went through the forest until she came to the seven dwarfs' house.

When the old woman knocked, Snow White called out, "I am not allowed to let anyone in."

"But I'm so very tired," the old woman said. "Let me in so I can rest."

Snow White could not refuse. She opened the door. Then the old woman offered Snow White the apple.

"I can't take it," Snow White replied.

"What are you afraid of?" asked the old woman. "Look, I will eat the white half, and you can eat the red." But the apple was cleverly made so that only the red cheek was poisoned.

Snow White longed to taste the tempting fruit. When she saw the peasant woman eating it herself, she couldn't resist. She took the poisoned half and bit into it.

But hardly had the first bite passed her lips then she fell down dead. Then the eyes of the cruel queen sparkled with glee. When she got home, she asked her mirror,

"Mirror, mirror, hanging there,
Who in all the land's most fair?"

And the mirror replied,

"My Queen in all the land I see
None as fine and fair as thee."

Only then was her jealous heart at peace.

When the dwarfs came home that evening, they found Snow White on the ground. They lifted her up and looked everywhere for anything poisonous, but all in vain. The girl was dead, and she remained dead.

The seven dwarfs wept over her for three days. At last they made up their minds to bury her. But she looked so lovely and rosy that they said, "We can't hide her away in the black ground."

So they laid her in a coffin made of glass. On the lid they wrote her name in golden letters to show that she was a royal princess.

Snow White lay in the coffin a long, long time, and she always looked the same, just as if she were fast asleep. She remained as white as snow, as red as blood, as black as ebony.

Now it happened that one day a prince came to the forest and passed by the dwarfs' house. He saw the coffin with the beautiful maiden inside it and read what was written in golden letters. "Give me the coffin," he said to the dwarfs. "I'll pay you whatever you like for it."

But the dwarfs said, "No, we wouldn't part with it for all the gold in the world."

"Then give it to me as a gift," said the prince, "because I can't live without Snow White." He spoke so sadly that the good dwarfs had pity on him and gave him the coffin. But as the prince's men lifted it, they stumbled. This jolted the coffin so violently that the poisoned bit of apple fell out of Snow White's throat. She opened her eyes and sat up.

The prince told her all that had happened. "I love you better than anyone in the whole wide world. Will you come to my palace and be my wife?"

Snow White consented with joy, and the marriage was arranged with great pomp and splendor.

Now Snow White's wicked stepmother was one of the guests invited to attend the wedding feast. But when she saw that the young bride was Snow White, she was so jealous that she choked with envy and died.

And Snow White and her prince lived and reigned happily over their kingdom for many, many years.